ESCAPE
from
COLD DITCH

Alan Davidson

ESCAPE
from
COLD DITCH

Illustrated by John Richardson

STRAW HAT

First published in 1995 by Straw Hat
This paperback edition first published 1997
Reprinted 2000

Printed and bound in Great Britain
by Hackman Print Group, Caerphilly
for the publisher,
Straw Hat

A CIP catalogue record for this book is available from the British Library

ISBN 1-899587-02-0

Contents

Contents

Chapter 1

FLEUR HEARS THE CALL

It was a warm, sunny Sunday morning on Farmer Stringroundknees' little farm. Primroses were out in the wood, lambs frisked, horses snorted, fledglings paraded their open beaks. Every bursting leaf-bud and sprouting branch and baby creepy-crawly awoke again to the exciting challenge of making itself the best leaf, the finest branch, the most OBNOXIOUS creepy-crawly. Life, life, life... It was spring, spring, spring...

From a clump of nettles by the stream came a satisfied cackle as Fleur, a handsome white hen, rose from laying an egg.

She glanced down briefly for a quality inspection. It was an egg to be proud of, big and thick-shelled and free-range, nutrition-full and salmonella free. A good egg.

From such as this came Farmer

Stringroundknees' reputation for producing nothing but the very best and Fleur had every right to be proud. Like every other hen on the farm she was devoted to 'the boss' and wanted to do her very best for him.

So, looking down at her egg, Fleur ought to have been thinking, quite simply: 'Another good day's work.' That was certainly what any other hen on the farm would have thought, but then, not to beat about the bush, your average hen is pretty feather-brained. Fleur was not feather-brained. She was a Hen of Vision and her first thought, after the cackle, was:

'This is not enough.'

Don't get it wrong. Fleur wasn't thinking she ought to produce *two* eggs a day. An obsessional urge for ever-greater productivity was no part of the way of life on Stringroundknees Farm. No, no. What she meant was that simply producing eggs was not enough. Not when you considered what was going on in the great world outside.

And to see that you only had to lift your beak. For the great world outside was

crowding in ever more closely. Look ahead and there, beyond the hawthorn hedge, was the Nodding Parva nuclear power station. To the left, on the other side of Primrose Wood, the Nodding Parva industrial estate and chemical complex. Over to the right, the motorway and Nodding Parva service station and, beyond them, the Nodding Parva Nature Reserve which consisted of a car park for two hundred cars, ten picnic benches, one information bureau staffed by four executives, numerous warning notices and overflowing litter bins and seven trees.

Only behind Fleur was there still a sort of countryside outside the farm. Every tree and hedge had, naturally, been removed and it rolled to the horizon dead, dead, dead with nothing to distract the eye.

Save for one thing. The great, sinister, silent, black shed in the distance.

The prison camp. Known as Cold Ditch Farm.

Fleur and her friends would discuss the prison camp in hushed squawks over evening forage.

Cold Ditch

'Kept squashed in cages. Can't even move.'

'Never feel the fresh air on their feathers. Not even an exercise yard.'

'Never see a woodlouse, never mind taste one.'

'Can't even roost properly.'

'The humans call it "battery farming". Trust them to give it a fancy name.'

And the hens would all cluck and lift their eyes to the heavens and feel very thankful they lived in a free farmyard.

'But,' Fleur would wonder - she being a Hen of Vision - 'for how long? Freedom must be fought for and we are not fighting.' She would brood about it while the others were roosting. But what could she do? It was true that she had certain special qualities, rare in a hen. From a vague desire to better herself and put time to good use she had long practised using her right claw to grip things with and pick them up. It was very difficult, especially as it meant having to balance on the other leg while doing so, and it wasn't easy to see what use it would be, but it had felt positive, somehow better than nothing.

Also, she had made a study of human speech and could now understand it pretty well, unlike the average hen who made no effort at all.

But was there any point in it? What was the use of knowledge for knowledge's sake? Oh dear! Being a Hen of Vision was so disturbing. How much more comfortable to be feather-brained!

'You look broody,' said Betty, joining Fleur as she stepped out of the nettles. Betty was one of the cheeriest of the hens, totally feather-brained but so good-natured. You couldn't help liking her. 'Thinking of a few little chicks, maybe?'

'I was wishing,' said Fleur, wistfully, 'that there was something I could do to save the world.'

'What from?'

'Oh, that and that and particularly that,' said Fleur, nodding around her.

'Now that's silly,' said Betty. 'A hen can't save the world. Anyway, you've got a full-time job here. If you went dashing off trying to save the world you'd have the boss on your tail.'

'I know, I know,' said Fleur wondering which, after all, was the more feather-brained, Betty or herself. She was, probably. Betty was the one with her claws on the ground; she the dreamer.

'Cheer up and have a woodlouse,' said Betty. 'Look, there are a couple of nice fat ones here. Or what about this bit of rotten potato peeling? It looks scrumptious, really mature. No, I insist . . .'

Betty

Betty was so kind. Fleur's eyes filled with tears as she thought of the hens in the prison camp. No friendly chatting and scratching for them. If only...

What could she do to take her mind off it? Of course - a little music. The sun was over the power station roof so it must be time for the club.

The Music Club was one of the nice little extras on Stringroundknees Farm. It had been for the plants originally. Farmer Stringroundknees had thought they'd like some music and grow better for it so he'd wired up the greenhouse for tapes. Then he'd noticed that some of the animals came to listen too so he'd turned up the volume. An hour every morning, with something for every taste. Pop, a little Mozart perhaps, opera, fifties and sixties songs for the older plants and animals. The cows would come close up to the hedge to lie down, dreamily chewing the cud or swishing their tails to the beat. The more thoughtful pigs would stand around with rapt looks on their faces. Several sheep came along, some ducks.

Fleur was the only hen to attend the club but even those who merely heard the music from a distance got something from it.

There happened to be a lot of opera that morning which pleased Fleur, who liked nice songs. It was very moving. Listening to *One Fine Day* from *Madame Butterfly* made her think again of the hens in the prison camp, waiting and longing for someone to come over the horizon to their rescue. Silly, perhaps, but it brought a tear to her eye.

The last notes died away. The cows and the pigs and the sheep and the ducks wandered off, leaving Fleur alone with her sad thoughts. She was about to go too when suddenly she heard her name spoken.

'Fleur,' said a voice. And, again, 'Fleur'. It was so strange that she gave a little squawk and a jump. It was in the air all around her. Where was it coming from? It sounded like Farmer Stringroundknees' voice but more...portentous...disembodied. It was as if all nature were speaking to her.

'Fleur,' it said. 'Oi believe ee are a special hen, a Hen of Vision that understands what oi say. Fleur, oi believe the time has come for ee to gird eeself, to take weapon in hand and help save the world.'

Fleur's beak fell open and she looked upwards, turning on the spot, trying to make out where the voice was coming from.

Or was she having delusions? Was it coming from inside her own head? There it was again.

'Ee are a special hen'

'Prove oi'm right in believing ee understands what I say. Prove it by reporting to the woodshed now.'

17

Then it dawned upon Fleur that the voice must be coming to her in the same mysterious way as the music. Through that machinery that humans have. Humans had machinery for everything.

'*Now, Fleur, now*. Oi be waiting.'

Was this how Joan of Arc had felt? As if in a trance, looking to neither left nor right, Fleur set off for the woodshed.

Chapter 2

SPECIAL AGENT OF THE RESISTANCE

The door was ajar. Fleur paused for a moment to peer in but it was quite dark inside and because of the contrast with the brilliant sunshine she could see nothing. Taking her courage in both claws, she entered.

From the gloom came a sigh of satisfaction and a voice said: 'Oi knew it. Oi knew ee were a Hen of Vision that understands what oi say.'

There was only one small window in the shed. It was partly hidden by the piles of logs and so grimy that it didn't let much light in anyway but as her eyes grew accustomed to the gloom Fleur saw that a face was silhouetted against it. Presumably the face belonged to someone sitting on the logs, someone who could see her much more clearly than she could see him because of the light coming in through the open door. It was a lumpy, craggy sort of face.

Farmer Stringroundknees had a lumpy, craggy sort of face.

From it jutted an unlit clay pipe, also silhouetted against the window.

Farmer Stringroundknees always had an unlit clay pipe sticking out of his mouth though he'd given up smoking it many years ago.

The voice sounded like that of Farmer Stringroundknees.

Otherwise, the identity of this person remained a mystery. He spoke again.

'Oi've been watching ee for some time now, Fleur. Ee are not like other hens. Give a squawk now to prove again that ee understands what oi say.'

Fleur squawked self-consciously and there came another satisfied sigh.

'And young and fit, too. Let me see ee jump to the top of these logs. In one bound.'

Fleur did so, producing yet another satisfied sigh.

'Cleanly done. Not an excess bit of flap or flutter. Oi have a need for a hen like ee. Ee can get down again now Fleur and oi'll tell ee why oi've brought ee here.'

Fleur dropped silently from the logs.

'First, though, oi want ee to swear an oath of secrecy. That whatever happens ee will never reveal to any person or animal what is said inside this HQ. Will ee swear that, Fleur? To do so, raise your right wing and squawk once.'

Fleur did so. She had a feeling of great excitement but she kept it under control because she felt it was important to appear disciplined.

'Good,' said the voice. 'And neither will ee think of me by my proper name which is too long for ee to get your thoughts round anyway. Oi will be known to ee only as "S". Is that understood?'

Fleur squawked again.

'Hexcellent. Now oi don't suppose ee reads the newspapers or the circulars from the Ministry of Agriculture' - Fleur flapped her wing dismissively (already communicating was becoming easier). 'But oi can tell ee this. Everywhere there are humans who care for nothing but money, or, putting it another way, getting the best return on their investment. And for that they'll put an end to all the nice little things of life. Ee knows what oi mean, don't ee, Fleur.'

Yes, she knew. Sharing an earwig with Betty. Dust baths on an autumn evening. The feel of rotten wood on your beak as you foraged for beetles.

'It's an attack on our souls, Fleur. And they take prisoners. Ee knows what lies over there?'

A big finger was suddenly silhouetted against the window, pointing into the distance towards that silent black shed. Cold Ditch.

'Hundreds of hens kept as slaves from the egg to the cull. How can we let them rot there, Fleur? It's long been on my mind to fight back, to form a resistance movement. But it's never been possible because oi didn't have the special agent oi needed to help. An insider. A hen who can get in there and mingle as one of them. A hen of resource and daring who can understand what oi say and obey orders and also use her own initiative. *And* - ' S's voice became even more meaningful - 'who can use her right claw for holding things.'

So that had been noticed, too. It wasn't useless, after all.

'Ee'll need further training but ee've got the basic skills. Sometimes oi've almost despaired, Fleur. Oi've waited many years to find a hen like ee. But at last oi have.'

A thrill ran through Fleur.

'Are ee willing to be a special agent for the Resistance, Fleur? Your first mission to penetrate that prison camp, organise the prisoners and help them escape? Bring them here to be dispersed to free farmyards up and down the country?'

Willing? It was what she had always instinctively yearned for!

'It would be ee against the world, Fleur. Ee'd be on your own, a free-ranging hen. Oi don't have to tell ee what might happen if ee were caught. Oi can't offer ee nothing but sweat, toil, tears and maybe - '

A hand was silhouetted against the window. It made a chopping motion.

'What do ee say, Fleur? Do ee accept the call?'

Fleur raised her head, proudly. And then - it was difficult but she did it - she raised her right claw part way towards it. It was a kind of salute.

'Ee'll go into special training, starting tomorrow,' said S. 'Parachuting, weaponry, general fitness with special attention to development of right claw, communication with human beings both normal and techno-techno - whatever the word is... It'll be hard, Fleur, but together we'll make a start. On saving the world.'

Chapter 3

BRAVE BATTERY OF HENS

While Fleur roosted and dreamed that evening in preparation for a hard day ahead, the hens of Cold Ditch Farm were having a sing-song, their beaks raised feebly as they warbled. The voice that could be heard above all the rest was that of Captain Curly.

> *Just beside the nestbox*
> *Near the henhouse gate*
> *Darling, I remember*
> *The way you used to wait*
> *'Twas there that you squawked,*
> > *so tenderly -*

'Oh, come on, chaps, do sing up,' said Captain Curly, breaking off. 'I've never heard such a lot of dismal quavering. Let's try another one and this time put some *go* in it.'

Goodbye, the old farmyard
Farewell, the fresh air
It's a long, long way to Farmer Giles's
But my heart's right there

Captain Curly

'Oh, I don't know...' It wasn't often that Captain Curly looked disheartened but she did now. 'We've got to *try* and stay cheerful.

Once we stop doing that we're finished. It's got to be never say die, beaks up, chests out. Why weren't you singing, Pankhurst?'

'Singing songs is all very well,' said a hen who'd been staying stubbornly silent, staring scornfully to one side and making little clucking noises. 'You know I normally sing up with the best but there comes a time when it's not enough. You've got to *do* something.'

'If you've got any suggestions,' said Captain Curly, wearily, 'we'd be pleased to hear them, wouldn't we chaps.'

(Officially, the hens didn't have names but they'd given them to each other. Captain Curly was called that because her tail-feathers curled and because she was a natural leader, always ready to take responsibility. Pankhurst was named after Mrs Pankhurst, the fiery-spirited suffragette who'd been so indomitable in prison).

There was a half-hearted murmur of agreement from some of the hens. The others just looked glum.

'Apathetic lot,' mumbled Pankhurst.

Pankhurst

'Sitting in this terrible place and not bothering to do anything about it.'

'If you'd just *say* what we could do, Pankhurst,' said Captain Curly. 'For a start, how can we get these cages open?'

'I'll think of something. Just give me time.'

'Shh!' another hen said sharply. 'Fat Martha.'

A hen came strutting along the gangway between the rows of cages, a swagger stick under her wing (really a bit of old cane she'd found). This hen, unlike the others, was plump, well-fed, bright-eyed and glossy. She was also free to move around, with her own private quarters at one end of the camp. Fat Martha was despised but also feared. A loud

Fat Martha

cackle from her or a pull with her beak at the cord by her perch would bring the Commandant (the human) to the scene. Let her eye then come to rest in an accusing glare on any unhappy hen and that hen might disappear to wherever it was that hens disappeared to when they were carried protesting away. No one liked to talk too much about that but in their hearts they knew. The dreaded cull. Yes, they knew. This practice of Fat Martha had a name. It was called 'giving the glare'.

Fat Martha was a collaborator, willing to sell her soul to the enemy for the sake of an easy life.

'What's all this racket?' she jeered. 'It woke me up. I wouldn't mind if you could sing but all that cackling was most unpleasant on the ear. Perhaps I'll give you a few lessons sometime, *if* you're lucky.' (Fat Martha fancied herself as a singer) 'What's that? Did I hear something?' (Pankhurst had given a long, low, jeering cluck) 'Was it Pankhurst? I think Pankhurst ought to watch out because she's in danger of getting another black mark and you all know what happens to hens who get too many black marks, don't you.'

There was a sombre silence.

'They get the glare, don't they. So, now we all know where we stand I'll get back to my comfy perch. See you anon, all you cool chicks.'

'I'll get her one day,' muttered Pankhurst, savagely. 'One day I'll get my beak into her tail-feathers and PULL. You'll see.'

'Squawk, squawk, squawk,' said Captain Curly, wearily. 'That's all you ever do. That's all any of us ever do.'

Captain Curly sagged and silence fell over the prison camp. Tomorrow would be another day. Just one more day in the life of an imprisoned hen.

'Sometimes,' thought Captain Curly, 'I feel at the end of my feather.'

Chapter 4

INTO THE TRAINING PROGRAMME

MONDAY: The first day of Fleur's fortnight of special training. She had been working hard since dawn and was now in the Long Meadow behind Primrose Wood making her first circuits of the assault course. *Leap* the fence, *scramble* up the netting, *balance* on the rope, *jump* to the top of the oil drum....she was going to be stiff that night.

Watching from the deep shadows of Primrose Wood was what appeared to be a heap of old waterproof clothing. From time to time, however, it moved and shouted hoarse words of encouragement. Also, from near the top where a mouth might be concealed, a clay pipe projected, at such a steep angle that had there been tobacco in the bowl it would have fallen out when the pipe waggled, as it did at every shout.

33

'Come on, Fleur,' cried S. 'Ee be doing fine. Stick it out.'

Her programme that day had gone like this:

Dawn till mid-morning break: Leg and claw exercises with special attention to standing on left leg while using right claw for gripping. Kept falling over.

Morning break till lunch: Theory of communication with humans; interpretation of commands, the principles of acknowledgement with use of squawk and cluck.

Afternoon: Assault course.

It was tough. But if you wanted to be a special agent you didn't expect things to be easy. You were trying to be the *crème de la crème.* Up, down, run, jump, stagger, push yourself on till the red glare appeared in front of your eyes...

'Just one more time, Fleur. Ee be doing fine.'

The approval in S's voice gave her the strength to carry on.

Yes, she knew that she would roost soundly that night.

Some highlights of the fortnight:

TUESDAY: Finer movements with right claw. Experimenting with picking up objects. Still falling over quite a lot.

First introduction to radio and pistol. Familiarisation only as yet. Claw still clumsy and fell over again.

'Rome weren't built in a day,' said S, soothingly.

And, of course, the assault course.

Run, jump, stagger, push yourself on

WEDNESDAY: Aching and stiffness at its worst today. Difficult to drag herself off her perch. Despairing at how much there was to learn. For the first time wondering if she would be able to do it, if the whole idea of a hen becoming a secret agent wasn't simply a mad dream. Somehow dragged herself through the day.

THURSDAY was no better.

FRIDAY: A thrilling day. Suddenly, everything was falling into place. She was full of bounce, zest, determination. And she was no longer falling over when she stood on one leg.

For the first time she was allowed to carry her pistol - in a tiny under-wing holster kept in place by a thread concealed beneath the feathers. Uncomfortable at first but she soon got used to it. She also pulled the trigger for the first time. When loaded, the pistol fired two pellets capable of knocking out for a while a human or animal. S had bought it at a special shop in London. It was, said S, for use only as a last resort.

SATURDAY: The beginnings of target practice. She was already a far leaner, fitter hen.

SUNDAY: Day of rest. Betty asked where she'd been for the past week and she mumbled vaguely that she'd been on 'special duties'. Betty was too feather-brained to ask what they were.

MONDAY: Use of radio and special tools.

TUESDAY: A big day. First parachute jump using a parachute made from one of Mrs Stringroundknees' old vests with arm- and neck-holes stitched up. The jump was from the shovel of a mechanical digger held up high. She landed successfully with barely a flap and walked away feeling three feet tall. She made several more jumps that day, each one higher than the last.

WEDNESDAY: Study sessions. Layout of prison camps, security measures, opposition to be expected. Dealing with doors, cage fastenings etc. Aspects of tunnelling.

THURSDAY and FRIDAY: Revision days. She now had a new-found confidence which sprang from an iron-hard physical fitness and skills possessed by no hen in history before her.

SATURDAY: Passing-out test. She sailed through it with flying colours.

'Ee be everything oi hoped for,' said S.

She was now a fully-fledged special agent. On Sunday morning she went to the woodshed for a final briefing and during the afternoon she rested.

Monday would see her skills and courage tested in action.

Chapter 5

THE HEN HAS LANDED!

Monday in the prison camp. Another boring fortnight had passed. Another fortnight of nothing happening apart from boring food coming along the boring conveyor belt, boring visits from the Commandant and boring bossing around and boasting from boring Fat Martha.

Since nobody felt like a sing-song, Captain Curly was encouraging the hens to tell folk-tales. One in particular, a studious and sensitive hen named Homer, had gathered a large collection of legends which had been passed down from generation to generation. One or two of the silliest hens (all hens being a *bit* silly) refused to believe anything about them at all and cackled and made facetious remarks, but most listened enthralled, if a little disbelieving.

'What have you got for us today then, Homer?' cackled one of the silliest hens, Kylie. 'Something about a monster, perhaps? A black monster with working wings that flew through the air and came down and sucked eggs. What was it called - CROW, was it? Or MAGPIE? No, MAGPIE was black and white, wasn't it.'

'I don't like monster stories,' said a saucy young hen called Marilyn. 'I like stories about the real world.'

'If this is what you mean by the real world,' said Pankhurst, bitingly, 'then nothing ever happens in it. So there aren't any stories.' Pankhurst loved the old legends.

'Well, I can't swallow all that make-believe,' clucked Marilyn. 'Stuff about *grass* and *sky* and *sun* and *rain* and all that rot.'

'Now don't you be so full of yourself,' said Captain Curly. 'There are more things in heaven and earth than are dreamed of by a young pullet like you. Who is to say that grass and sky and sun and rain did not exist, do not exist, even now, somewhere outside this camp? Personally, I'm a believer. I think they do. Behind all legend lies reality.'

'So shut your beak and listen,' said Pankhurst, whose cage was between Marilyn and Kylie, 'or I'll give you a peck in the ear. Carry on Homer and squawk up nice and loud because it's not easy for everyone to hear.'

'Today,' said Homer, 'I'm going to tell you the greatest of all folk-tales, that of Ermintrude and the Fox.'

A little shudder ran down the ranks of hens.

'Fox!' repeated a timid hen called Ethel.

Ethel

41

She found the very name frightening.

'The greatest, most ruthless of the monsters of old. The very king of monsters. My story takes place in the dim days of prehistory when, as someone said, there was grass and sky and sun and rain - '

'Tell us again what grass was like,' breathed Pankhurst, eagerly.

'It covered the floor everywhere and was like endless soft, juicy spikes that rippled in what was called the breeze and it was lovely and green and delicious to eat and - '

'What was green?' asked Marilyn, just to be difficult.

'That has to be a matter for some speculation - '

'You don't know.'

' - but as I said it was lovely and there were other juicy plants mixed in with it, dandelions for instance, and all sorts of scrumptious little tit-bits crawling about in it, just there for the taking - '

'Big rock candy mountain,' tittered Marilyn.

'Paradise,' agreed Pankhurst, dreamily, so

carried away she didn't realise Marilyn was mocking. 'The Garden of Eden!'

'I suppose,' said Ethel, timidly, 'a fox would think the same thing. And to a fox, we would be - er - part of the candy.'

'Undoubtedly the most luscious part,' nodded Homer. 'And there was one fox mightier than all the others, the biggest, most fearsome of all foxes with dripping jaws' - more shudders - 'and huge forepaws that could send the earth flying and tunnel deep under any fence into a chicken run' - squawks of horror - 'and if anybody asks "What was a chicken run?" I shall burst my gizzard because you really ought to know a bit of ancient history by now.'

'What was this fox's name?' asked Pankhurst.

'Just Fox. With a capital F. He was so terrible that he represented all foxes. All hens lived in fear of him. And then - Ermintrude appeared.'

'Ermintrude,' breathed Pankhurst.

'Just a humble hen of no privileged background. Hatched in a slum of a dried-up ditch. Quiet, unassuming, always waiting politely in the queue for the food-hopper. But there was nothing ordinary about her courage and determination. Behind the gentle exterior lay a spirit of grit. Almost straight from the egg she had an inner conviction that she was born for greatness, that she had a mission and when the call came she must be ready. Quietly she trained herself to use her right claw for picking things up, the first hen ever to do so.'

There was a squawk of derision from Kylie.

'That really is ridiculous,' said Marilyn. 'As if any hen could pick things up in her right claw like a human. I've never heard of anything so soft. I - '

She was silenced by a menacing glare from Pankhurst, but, in any case, here we must break into Homer's telling of the legend because outside the prison camp momentous events were taking place.

In the gathering darkness a machine was approaching from the direction of Stringroundknees Farm, a mechanical digger, the great shovel raised to its full height on vertical steel arms. Slowly, relentlessly, it ground along the narrow road and into the lane leading to the camp. Hunched in the driving seat was the shapeless mass we know to be S, clay pipe jutting out almost vertically from where the mouth might be.

Inside the shovel, high above the ground, was Fleur, parachute on, pistol in under-wing holster, bag containing vital equipment strapped to her body by a second under-feather thread. As they penetrated ever deeper into enemy territory she was quiveringly on the alert for any sign of movement ahead. Now they were nearing the Commandant's house. If S's intelligence reports were correct, he ought to be indoors at supper at this time but in this game of hide and seek, of life and death, you could take nothing for granted.

They were nearing the camp itself. She tensed, waiting for the signal which would send her into action.

She had been through it all in training. This was for real.

'It was,' continued Homer, 'after a particularly terrible attack by Fox that Ermintrude heard the call of Destiny. She had perfected the use of her right claw and suddenly, in a sort of vision, she saw what she must do with her skill.

'It was a freezing winter's morning with

snow on the ground. During the night Fox, no doubt driven on by a great hunger, had dug his longest tunnel ever, right into Ermintrude's own henhouse. He had savagely killed many hens and carried off a

The great Ermintrude follows the call of Destiny

charming young pullet called Athene who was loved by all.

'All the rest of that night there had been terrible anguish and pandemonium because you know how helpless we hens feel. We are not equipped to fight or take revenge. Nobody fears us. It is enraging.

'And then, suddenly, calmly, Ermintrude announced that she was going after Fox. She intended to challenge him to a duel to the death. They all tried to stop her, of course, they said she was mad, that hens were not made to resist, that no hen could challenge Fox, even a hen that could use her right claw. "What," they asked her, "is your weapon?"

'"My weapon," she answered, proudly, "is myself."

'Since then, of course, these words have become some of the most famous and oft-quoted in all hen mythology but then they seemed silly. They begged her to be sensible but she wouldn't listen.

'"A hen's got to do," she said, "what a hen's got to do."

'And she set off through the same tunnel that Fox had dug. Because of the snow she was able to follow his tracks, under hedges and across streams, through dark woods where lurked wild mink and weasel and other foxes, all the monsters of old, till finally she came to Fox's lair which was called *earth*...'

Outside in the near darkness of the moonless night the great digger had stopped close beside the perimeter fence. The engine had been switched off and in the sudden uncanny silence an owl hooted. At the prearranged signal - a twitch of the shovel - Fleur perched on one of the great steel teeth. Then, summoning up her courage, she leapt...

Her parachute streamed out behind her, the air ballooning it into the shape of an old vest - which is what it was, of course. A heart-stopping moment as she wondered if she had made a misjudgment and would fail to clear the fence - then the earth was rushing to meet her and with a flap and a flap and a flutter she was rolling over...

The hen had landed. She was inside the prison compound, the fenced-off area with its locked gate. Now she had to get inside the

The hen has landed

great shed itself but her training had taught her how to do that...

There was a roar from behind as S

restarted the engine. As the sound receded into the distance, Fleur knew that she was on her own.

'...and listening by the entrance to Fox's earth,' continued Homer, 'Ermintrude could hear Fox laughing and boasting to other foxes about the super meal he'd brought home alive. By that of course he meant that charming young pullet, Athene. It's the disgusting way that monsters used to talk. And then...Ermintrude called down into the hole.

'"Fox," she called, "I am Ermintrude the Hen and I have come to challenge you to a fight to the death. The prize is to be Athene."

'Fox couldn't at first believe his ears but when he popped his nose out to have a look he laughed and laughed and said of course he accepted the challenge and how nice it was to have a second hen for supper without having had the bother of carrying it home. He was laughing so much he couldn't get out of the hole.'

'I'm not surprised,' cackled Kylie.

Pankhurst made a lunge at her with her beak but wasn't quite quick enough.

'Well, this is all soft as well,' said Marilyn. 'Hens using their claws and going on missions. I ask you!'

'I think she was terrific,' breathed Pankhurst. 'I could follow a hen like that.'

'Please don't interrupt,' said Captain Curly. 'Let Homer tell the story.'

But Homer was suddenly staring fixedly, craning her neck to peer along the gangway. Other hens were doing the same.

'Yes, do go on, Homer,' said Pankhurst. 'What have you stopped for?'

Homer suddenly began speaking very rapidly.

'She - er - she used one of her own feathers to tickle his nose. Fox just kept rolling around laughing - fell in river - drowned. Ermintrude died tragically in snow on way back - Athene lived to tell the tale - '

But she had lost interest altogether. Everyone had lost interest except Pankhurst and when she looked round she lost interest too.

'I come from the free world'

A strange hen was squeezing her way in through the partially opened door. A bag was somehow strapped round her body and she was using her right claw to keep the door open.

A silence had fallen. Not a squawk nor a cluck nor a rustle. Now the hen was inside and the door was swinging to behind her. She faced her audience boldly, as she had been taught.

'I am Free-Ranging Fleur, Resistance Fighter,' she said, clearly and firmly. 'I have come to help you escape.'

Chapter 6

THE ESCAPE COMMITTEE MEETS

Captain Curly was the first to find her voice.

'Come from where, may I ask?' she squawked.

'From the Free World. From Stringround-knees Farm where you'll be offered a safe house before being passed on to other, friendly farms. There's good green grass waiting for you with fresh woodlice and grubs, excellent defences against foxes - all will be welcome.'

Marilyn's beak had fallen open, as had a lot of other beaks.

'Did you say *grass*?' she said.

'*Green* grass?' squawked Pankhurst, triumphantly.

There was a prolonged hush, then a sudden babble. Nothing of interest had ever happened in the camp before and now - this!

A visitor from another world. It was Captain Curly who, as always, showed a cool head and easy authority.

'Quietly, chaps. Let's have some order.'

Recognising her as the natural leader she had been instructed to look out for, Fleur made her way along the gangway to stand below her cage.

'What evidence can you show us,' said Captain Curly, 'that what you say is true? You may simply be a fantasist, an escapee from some other camp driven crazy by the conditions there and babbling nonsense. How could you possibly help us to escape? We can't even get out of these cages. How would you set about that for a start, eh?'

Fleur had been ready for just this. Without a word she leapt up on to the food conveyor belt. S had shown her how to deal with each type of cage fastening. This was an easy one. She tapped at the catch with her beak and it sprang open.

'Now push,' she said.

Gingerly, Captain Curly pushed forward against the cage door. It moved outwards and upwards, being hinged at the top.

'Great Ermintrude!' she whispered. 'I could get out if I wanted.'

'And then you could let others out. I'll show you. Getting you out of the cages is no problem - it's getting out of the camp that's difficult - '

'*Cave*,' hissed Pankhurst. 'Fat Martha!'

There had been a sudden yawning cackle from Fat Martha's private quarters. Fortunately she was hidden behind a curtain but she could appear at any moment.

'Quick,' said Captain Curly. 'There's an empty cage opposite.'

Swiftly, Fleur pushed Captain Curly's door shut again. Two flaps and she was pecking at the catch of the cage door opposite. Hardly had she backed inside and pulled it to, using her beak, when Fat Martha appeared, yawning.

'Was I dreaming or was I not dreaming?' she said. 'Did I hear some sort of commotion? You weren't trying to enjoy yourselves, I hope - ?' Seeing Fleur, she halted.

*'You weren't trying to
enjoy yourselves, I hope?'*

'Who are you?' she said. 'I seem to
remember this cell was empty.'

'A new prisoner,' said Captain Curly,
hastily. 'Commandant just brought her in.
We were saying hello, weren't we chaps.'

There was a general cackle of agreement
though some hens, Ethel among them,
looked frightened.

'Unusual,' said Fat Martha, looking up at
Fleur suspiciously. 'A single new prisoner?
And you look different - healthy. Who are
you? Got a name?'

59

Fortunately, from her angle Fleur's bag was out of sight, squashed as it was against the back of the cage. And the fact that the cage wasn't properly fastened wasn't obvious. Even so...

'Yes, Ma'am. They call me Fleur.'

Fat Martha found that "Ma'am" very pleasing. It wasn't often she got any respect.

'Fleur, let me introduce you,' said Captain Curly. 'This is Fa - this is Martha. She's in charge of us. She looks a bit - well - ruthless (Fat Martha's chest feathers puffed out importantly at this) but she's not so bad underneath.'

'I wouldn't be too sure about that,' said Fat Martha. 'I wouldn't be too sure at all. I'm known as a bit of a hard case. You won't find it easy to put one over on me.'

'She's also,' said Captain Curly, 'a talented singer. 'You might have a chance of hearing her.'

'I'll look forward to that,' said Fleur. 'I'm a music lover myself. I can very much see you in the role of Carmen if you don't mind me saying so.'

'Well, you never know your luck.' Fat Martha was by now in benevolent mood and had forgotten any thoughts of asking the Commandant about the new arrival. 'Keep your beak clean and you may have that privilege.'

She swaggered off back to her roost and there was a general cackle of relief. A few minutes later a snore was heard.

'Phew! That was a close shave,' said Captain Curly. 'Still we're safe enough now. She'll sleep for hours. Look, I won't be able to get off for excitement, I don't know about the rest of you.'

'Course we won't,' burst out Pankhurst, who'd kept herself under control as long as this only because she hadn't known what to talk about first - the escape, or the fabulous world outside the camp. There were so many questions to ask that even now her beak just opened and stayed there, making gurgling noises.

'I think,' said Fleur, who was the calmest hen there, thanks to her training, 'that there's not a moment to lose. I think you

61

'Of course we've all got gizzards for the escape'

should immediately elect an escape committee so that we can lay plans. First, though, I must warn you - this won't be easy. There'll be great danger and any hen with no gizzard for the escape is entitled to stay behind. All I ask is that you do not betray the rest of us.'

'Of course we've all got gizzards for the escape,' squawked Pankhurst, finding her voice. 'It's what we've always yearned for.

Let's get this committee elected. I propose Captain Curly as Chair and if anyone wants to propose me as a member - I accept.'

Within minutes the newly formed committee was gathering in a corner of the shed at the furthest point from Fat Martha's quarters. Their beaks were still open from the surprise of it all. Leaving her bag in her cage, Fleur had tapped open catches and, one by one, after flexing their muscles to make sure they still worked at least a little bit, the committee had flapped down and made their way along the gangway, watched by incredulous hens. The committee consisted of Captain Curly (Chair), Pankhurst and Homer. Fleur assumed the role of Secretary. It was a small committee but, as Fleur insisted, 'Small committees make for quick decisions'.

And by the time they had returned to their cages that night they had hatched out their plan. They would go into action the following night as soon as Fat Martha was asleep.

It was a long time before Pankhurst slept that night. She spent much of the time gazing across at Fleur.

'It's a privilege to be alive at one of the great moments in poultry history,' she thought. 'A new, greater Ermintrude is in our midst, in the cage opposite mine. She has come to deliver us.'

But not every hen felt so. Even in sleep Marilyn's expression was disbelieving. Secret agents telling ridiculous stories could arrive by the hundred as far as she was concerned. Nothing would ever convince *her* that all this make-believe about sun and earth and green grass and the rest of it held the least grain of truth. Common sense said it wasn't possible. How would it have got there? And what would be the point of it all when nobody ever saw it? No, no. Crackpots like Homer and this Fleur character could tell legends till they were blue in the beak but they wouldn't fool her.

And meanwhile Ethel was squawking in *her* sleep. She had wanted to ask Fleur to tell them not only about green grass and so on but also about foxes and crows and rats and weasels and all the other prehistoric

64

monsters and whether they still lived on but she hadn't the courage and now she dreamt about them. They were all pursuing her, monsters coming at her from every direction, closing in upon her as she twisted and turned in terror.

Other hens squawked in their sleep, too.

Chapter 7

CRY FREEDOM!

The plan was for a tunnel running beneath the shed wall and the perimeter fence. There was no other way. Unfortunately, there was only one place for it to start - under the floorboards directly below Fat Martha's sleeping quarters. Fleur had worked out that this was the only point where the perimeter fence came close enough for the plan to be practical.

There would be noise. But the committee had planned for that, too.

Even so, it would be a long tunnel, a mighty challenge for hens unused to scratching or any physical exercise.

During the day, Fleur saw the Commandant for the first time. Every hen froze as he looked in on a tour of inspection. Was it the cull? There came a sigh of relief as he left again. Otherwise she spent the rest of the time learning to live as a prisoner, doing nothing, squashed in her tiny cage, eating her rations, getting used to the humiliation of being unable even to turn around.

'What,' she said at one point, 'have you done to deserve this?'

'Nothing,' said Captain Curly, sadly. 'We have committed no crimes, injured no-one. That is the injustice of it all.'

There was, of course, a stream of eager questions about grass and sky and sun and rain and earth and insects and grubs but...

'It's no use,' said Fleur. 'I am a secret agent, not a poet. I cannot describe these things. You'll have to wait till you see for yourself.'

Marilyn continued to look amusedly to one side. Once or twice Ethel opened her beak but said nothing.

The excitement did not go unnoticed by Fat Martha.

'What's got into you lot?' she said, suspiciously, during her morning swagger down the gangway. 'You're like a lot of old washerwomen.'

The hens didn't mind this at all. There was a general cackle.

'We've been making plans, haven't we, chaps,' said Captain Curly.

'What do you mean, plans? How can you horrible lot have plans for anything?'

'Oh, you'll see what they are in good time,' said Captain Curly.

'Though you may not see *us*,' cackled Pankhurst. This was going too far and earned a warning look from Captain Curly though Fat Martha was now swaggering off along the gangway and so didn't hear.

'Well, just watch it,' she said. 'Watch it and keep your beaks clean or some of you might get the glare.'

That night when Fat Martha disappeared to her quarters every ear was straining for the first snore.

'There it goes,' said Pankhurst. 'She's off. Let's get started.'

But first, Fleur had certain duties to carry out. With her right claw she managed to

A technological hen

wriggle her bag forward in her cage. Watched closely by every hen who could see her she took from it a small black instrument with a short rod sticking from it. She pressed a little switch on the side.

'Come in Fleur,' said a voice. It was a radio. 'Be ee making your first report?'

A single squawk from Fleur.

'Everything satisfact'ry?'

Another squawk.

'Report progress again same time tomorrow. Over and out.'

Fleur pressed the switch again and returned it to the bag.

'A technological hen,' breathed Pankhurst.

'With Fleur on our side,' said Captain Curly, 'we hens can at last fight back against the world. We are no longer powerless. I just hope' - she glanced severely along the gangway - 'there are no traitors in our midst. No, I'm sure there aren't. I've never known a finer lot of chaps.'

And now came perhaps the most vital part of all. If this failed the whole plan would have to be abandoned. Taking a small metal lever from her bag, Fleur left her cage and flapped quietly down into the gangway.

'Good hunting,' said Captain Curly, briefly. She knew, as did every other hen watching, how much depended on this.

Fleur put the lever down and began inspecting floorboards. She was looking for a loose one or, at least, one with a weakness she could take advantage of, preferably at some distance from Fat Martha's quarters. She gradually worked her way along the gangway and disappeared from Captain Curly's view.

The hens waited. In the mind of every one

was the question: 'What happens if there is no loose floorboard?'

Fleur came scurrying back.

'There's one that's a bit loose.'

She picked up the lever, went off again. The waiting hens heard creaks.

'Is "a bit loose" loose enough?' wondered Captain Curly.

Fleur had inserted the lever into the crack between boards. The loose one strained. But a hen, even a hen as fit as Fleur, doesn't have much strength. She perched on the end of the lever, pressed down...jumped...and again...

Captain Curly heard the sudden wrenching noise, followed by a squawk of triumph. The first major obstacle had been overcome.

A few minutes later the first group of volunteer scratchers, led by Pankhurst, had been let out of their cages. On unsteady legs they stumbled along the gangway to flap down, one by one, through the gap in the floorboards.

Most went with little squawks of fright and wonder because even this was a new world.

There was something called Earth which none had experienced before. It had a smell and a touch they weren't used to. Fleur had to help some with their first faltering steps though Pankhurst contemptuously refused her offer and indeed did some helping of her own and was generally an inspiration, cajoling, issuing commands, sometimes bullying.

Helped by a little light that filtered its way down, Fleur led the way beneath the floorboards to the spot where they were to dig. There, they were to wait till she gave the signal to scratch.

When Fleur popped her head above the floorboards again she had an electrifying message to pass on.

'What's she say?' said Captain Curly, who was impatiently waiting for her part in the action to begin.

'Pankhurst has found a worm,' said Homer, faintly.

A worm! A prehistoric creature good to eat. The news ran from end to end of the camp.

'Well,' said Captain Curly, looking at

Marilyn, 'perhaps the unbelievers will now believe.'

'I'd like to see it,' said Marilyn, cynically. 'Can you ask Pankhurst to pass it up.'

'I'll ask,' said Fleur.

'Sorry, she's eaten it,' she reported a few moments later. 'It was delicious.'

'Huh!' said Marilyn.

But Fleur had too much to do to spend time chatting. Before the scratching could start, the problem of noise had to be dealt with. She opened more cages, starting with Captain Curly's.

Fat Martha woke to a sound of general

Pankhurst meets her firs
prehistoric creature

74

movement and cackling.

'What's going on out there at this time of night?' she muttered. 'I knew they were up to something. They can't put one over on me.'

Leaving her perch she strutted out into the gangway - and saw something so astonishing, so amazing, that she had to close her eyes tightly and open them again to make sure she wasn't dreaming. Several hens, including the new hen Fleur and Captain Curly, were standing chatting.

Her beak fell open.

'Oh, hello,' said Captain Curly. 'We were hoping we wouldn't disturb you. Sorry about this.'

'What are you doing outside your cages?' asked Fat Martha, faintly. '*How* did you get out?'

'Oh, that? Yes, I suppose it does look a bit odd. The Commandant happened not to shut mine properly so I got out and then opened the others. Easy-peasy, really. We could have got out before but we've never bothered. We like it in our cages, don't we

*'We're organising
a camp concert'*

chaps. Cosy. It's just that we've got a special purpose now.'

'Sp - special purpose?'

Captain Curly looked about her, as if to make sure no-one could overhear, before speaking confidentially.

'We're organising a camp concert. Secretly. Special surprise for the Commandant. Anniversary of his appointment, you know.'

'Anniversary?'

'Yes, I thought you'd know that.'

'Of course I knew. But - ' Fat Martha drew herself up. 'I can't have this. If you want to get out of your cages and have a concert you'll have to get the Commandant's permission first.'

'We can't do that,' said Captain Curly.

'Why not?'

'Spoil the surprise.'

Fat Martha looked confused.

'We wouldn't want to get you into trouble for spoiling the Commandant's surprise, would we chaps?' There was a chorus of agreement. 'We've a great respect for you though you're such a hard case.'

'Well, certainly, that's what I always say,' said Fat Martha. 'I always say you hens don't respect weakness. Boot 'em around, I say, and you'll get their loyalty.'

'Exactly,' nodded Captain Curly. 'Firmness mixed with knowing just when to give them their 'orrible 'eads a little bit. Before coming in with the boot again. That's what we respect, isn't it, chaps?' There was another cackle of agreement.

'Yes, well, just this once I'll give you your horrible heads a little bit. I wouldn't want to spoil the Commandant's surprise. But if you're going to have a concert it'd better be a good one or a few of you might get the glare. Is that understood?'

'We'll rehearse every night.'

'You'd better. And once the concert's over you'll be back in your cages again.'

And Fat Martha went back to her roost in the sure knowledge that she had handled a tricky situation with her usual flair. Drifting off to sleep she heard the hens' voices raised in chorus as they rehearsed just by her den.

> *There'll be lots-of-hens over*
> *The barbed wire enclosure*
> *Tomorrow just you wait and see.*
> *There'll be love and laughter*
> *And free woodlice ever after*
> *Tomorrow, when the hens are free.*

It masked the sound of the scratching now taking place immediately beneath her.

Hearing her snores, Fleur took a quick peep at her. Fat Martha roosted on her perch like some gross, slobbering Roman emperor, around her the visible signs of her pampered depravity. Spilled rations lay on the floor mixed up with old feathers. The place was a slum. Propped against the back wall was a picture. It was of Fat Martha herself looking bloated and smug, probably taken by the Commandant and given to her as a reward for her services.

'Your days are numbered,' thought Fleur with satisfaction. 'Soon, with luck, you will be swept into the dustbin of history.' And turning back to the other hens, Fleur squawked fiercely: 'Cry freedom!'

'Freedom!' Captain Curly and all the other hens squawked back in unison.

Fat Martha snored on.

Chapter 8

THE DANGEROUS CHARMS
OF FAT MARTHA

Wednesday night:

'Come in, Free-Ranging Fleur. Come in, Fleur. Are ee receiving me?'

Squawk.

'Is everything proceeding according to plan?'

Two squawks.

'Oh. Two squawks for "no", eh? Now oi wonder why?'

It was the following evening and Fleur was reporting to Control again. The scratchy sound was probably S rubbing his chin.

'Oi wonder, Fleur? Is the tunnel too long for the labour force available? Are the hens too weak from being imprisoned, you reckon?'

Squawk.

'Hah! Oi did think that might be a problem.

Try moles, Fleur. Understand? Moles.'

Squawk.

'Good luck, Free-Ranging Fleur... Over and out.'

Yes, there were problems. At the rate the teams of hens were scratching it would take years to dig a tunnel.

Also, Fleur was worried by the attitude of a few of the hens. Ethel, for instance, kept on nervously asking about foxes and other monsters. She was trying to catch Fleur's eye again now. More about monsters?

'Fleur.'

'Yes, Ethel?'

'Weren't there a lot of illnesses and - er - diseases in the old world? Fowlpest, bumblefoot - things like that?'

'Hypochondriac!' jeered Pankhurst. 'You can get diseases in here as well. Worse ones. *And* stress problems. I feel it myself. I get great urges to peck other hens.'

'They protect us in here,' said Ethel, timidly. 'They give us medicines.'

'Oh yes, protection from the egg to the cull. That's why the water tastes so nasty.'

'You needn't worry, Ethel,' said Fleur, soothingly. 'You'll feel a lot better outside, you really will.'

But Ethel didn't look convinced. Outside was...unknown.

'I'm not sure I want to be outside,' she said, but so quietly and timidly that only Fleur heard her.

It was worrying. Apart from anything else there was always the possibility that some hen, perhaps Ethel, might betray the rest of them, not maliciously but out of simple panic.

Later the same evening:

Moles aren't easy to get hold of. It takes a lot of squawking into holes and hoping they're within earshot.

Fortunately, when you do make contact, no animal is more obliging. Anyway, they like tunnelling. It's second nature to them. Any excuse.

So it didn't take long to fix things up. Getting them pointed in the right direction took most of the time.

It felt quite strange to be out in the open air again, the breeze in the prison yard ruffling her feathers. Pankhurst had begged to be allowed out with her but Fleur had insisted on patience. Discipline had to be strict. Allow one out and the others would clamour to follow. Captain Curly understood that.

Oh - the other thing was - Fleur saw a fox. They looked at each other through the netting. The fox appeared surprised at first,

'Hello'

standing motionless with one paw raised. Then a slow, knowing leer crossed his face. Fleur knew what he was thinking. She flirted her tail at him, secure behind the wire. Then she went back inside.

Saturday night:

'Come in, Fleur, come in Fleur. Are ee receiving me?'

Squawk.

'Did ee try moles?'

Squawk.

'Well done, Fleur. Are they any good?'

Squawk, squawk.

A thoughtful silence. Then:

'Oi suppose they don't make wide enough holes. No way of joining 'em together? Several moles digging side by side?'

Squawk, squawk.

'Oi suppose not. It was only a thought.'

Another, long silence. A *very* long silence.

'You *could* try a fox, Fleur. Understand?'

Another long silence. Even longer.

Squawk.

'Best of luck, Fleur. Over and out.'

Monday night:

'Good evening,' called Fleur. 'Have you time for a word?' The fox halted.

It was the same fox she had seen on Thursday evening. She had been waiting for him for two nights.

'Did I hear aright?' he asked. 'Did you say you'd like a word?'

'I did,' said Fleur, trying hard not to tremble.

'It's not often a hen addresses a fox so courteously.'

'It's not often a hen gets a chance. This fence makes for easy social intercourse.'

'It's a great leveller,' agreed the fox. They laughed together.

'I wanted to ask you something,' said Fleur. 'Something which has been puzzling me.'

'I am all attention.'

'You're a big strong fox. Daring, too, I'd say. And here's this prison full of hens yet you never try to get inside.'

'I shouldn't underestimate the difficulties,' said the fox, 'even for a digger like me and, yes, I agree, I'm no mean performer - '

'I think you could do it.'

' - but, anyway, what's the point?' The fox came close and sat down by the wire. Fleur could have touched him if she'd wanted to but she didn't want to. 'Er - I'm not used to talking to hens. I don't want to say anything which is socially unacceptable.'

'You can speak freely with me. I am unshockable.'

'Well, it's not worth it. The hens in these prisons are all skin and bone. Anyway, that's what I'm told. That's the gossip in the earths. Though, I must say...' He ran a slightly puzzled eye over Fleur.

'Don't believe everything you hear,' said Fleur. She looked around to make sure they were unobserved. 'Cast an eye on this.'

She took something from beneath her wing and showed it to the fox.

'Phew-ee!' said the fox, admiringly. And then - 'Wow!'

'Ever seen anything so alluring? Such plumpness! Such...*oomph*! Her name's Fat Martha.'

*'I could go for a
hen like that'*

Fleur had removed the picture while Fat
Martha was snoring.

'She's in the prison right behind me. What
do you think of her?'

'Let's just say...I could go for a hen like
that.'

They laughed together again.

'So, you see, these gossiping friends of
yours don't know everything, do they.'

'But may I ask,' said the fox, 'why you're
telling me this?'

'You and Fat Martha seem made for each
other. I thought you might be interested in a
meeting. If you did think of tunnelling into
the prison I could be a very useful go-
between. I can show you the exact point to

aim for and I can have a floorboard up all ready and waiting...'

The fox was eyeing her with frank suspicion. 'I don't get this,' he said. Then his expression changed. 'I see,' he said, knowingly, 'you've got something against her.'

'She's a collaborator with the authorities. All the hens loathe her.'

'I *see*... Well, anything to oblige. You say you'll help with the necessary arrangements...'

'No bringing friends.'

'Cub's honour. There's only enough for one, anyway. Oops! Pardon.'

'Granted. Let's make plans.'

'It's playing with fire,' said Captain Curly.

'There's no other way,' said Fleur.

'Course there's no other way,' squawked Pankhurst. 'If we don't take chances, we're done for.'

The escape committee was in emergency session. Fleur had called the meeting after replacing the picture while Fat Martha still snored. They were in a quiet spot at the end of the gangway. Far away at the other end a dance troupe was noisily rehearsing outside Fat Martha's quarters.

'If Ermintrude could deal with Fox,' said Pankhurst, 'we know *you* can with all your modern technology. And with us by your side.'

'Not quite by your side, perhaps,' said Homer, 'but fairly close behind.'

'How long does he estimate it'll take him to dig the tunnel?' asked Captain Curly.

'Two night job. E.T.A. around the middle of Wednesday night.'

'Wednesday,' breathed Pankhurst. 'The day that will go down in poultry history. On that day freedom's flame will once more burn brightly.'

'Till then,' said Fleur, 'scratching parties must continue as normal. So must the rehearsals so as to drown the noise. Only we, the committee, must know about Fox until the very last moment. To do otherwise would be to risk panic. At the very least, with hens merely idly waiting, there could be a slackening of resolve, even dissension.'

'You're right, of course,' said Captain Curly, sombrely, but...' she put her head on one side and looked at Fleur... 'it's a dangerous game.'

'Nothing worthwhile was ever achieved without danger,' said Fleur.

'And what about Fat Martha?' clucked Homer.

'What about her?' jeered Pankhurst.

'She's a fellow hen,' said Captain Curly, 'however contemptible. Can we really throw her to the foxes, to coin a phrase?'

There was a derisive squawk from Pankhurst.

'Now this really is sentimental tosh. It's not just prehistoric thinking. It's primeval, straight out of the days when they talked about sportsmanship and straight bats. It's pre-McEnroe. The world's moved on.'

Captain Curly looked unhappy.

'Pankhurst is right,' said Fleur, quietly. 'This is no time for sentiment. We must be as ruthless as the enemy. Only when we are free can we afford to be civilised again.'

Fleur was surprised at herself. She had learned her new trade well.

Captain Curly sighed. 'I suppose so. Perhaps I'm finding it difficult to think straight. I'm so tired...we all must be tired, up every night making plans, supervising the digging, the rehearsals...'

'Include me in that,' said Homer.

'...and two more nights still to go. But what worries me most is Fat Martha. Can she really keep on taking that racket just by her perch every evening? I know she's a heavy sleeper but *look*...'

The committee gazed along the gangway. The dance troupe were shuffling about pretending to rehearse, clucking and squawking.

'What a rabble!' cackled Pankhurst. 'I'm glad I'll never have to see this show.'

'Also,' said Captain Curly, 'I know Fat Martha's not very bright - thick as a henhouse post to be blunt about it - but surely even she must realise there's something...well...not *logical* in what we're doing. Surely it will dawn on her.'

There was a sudden screech from the far end of the gangway. Fat Martha came flouncing out of her quarters and the dancers scattered in confusion, squawking and clucking.

'Clear off,' squawked Fat Martha. 'I've had you lot right up to the gizzard so clear off. If you must rehearse why does it have to be

right by my roost? Go and make your vile din at the other end of the camp. NOW GET GOING.'

'It's just dawned on her,' nodded Captain Curly, dismayed. 'Exactly as I feared.'

'We have to do something,' said Fleur.

Chapter 9

DIG, DIG, DIG FOR VICTORY

Fleur led the committee along the gangway.

'Is anything the matter, Ma'am?' asked Captain Curly. 'We heard the commotion. We hope nothing's wrong.'

'Oh, it's you,' said Fat Martha. 'I'll say there's something wrong. I've told this lot to clear off and you can make sure they do. There I was on my perch and I suddenly thought: "If this lot has to rehearse, why does it have to be right by my ear? All the rest of the camp available and they choose this spot." They're stupid, that's their trouble, feather-brained and stupid. You, too.'

'I'm sorry,' said Captain Curly, haggardly. 'I'm afraid we're not used to organising shows and - '

'May I say something,' said Fleur, timidly.

'I know I'm a new prisoner, but - '

'Speak up,' said Captain Curly. 'All prisoners are equal here!'

'Equally horrible,' sneered Fat Martha.

'With Ma'am's permission, of course.'

'Hurry up then. I want to get back to my perch.'

'The concert committee - of which, as you can see, I am a member - has been thoughtless but we've had a lot of problems. You see, the show lacks a star, a centre-piece for it to revolve around. Isn't that so, Captain Curly?'

'Oh, yes. Big problem, this. Trying to make a silk purse out of a lot of sows' ears. We just haven't the *talent*.'

'You were saying to me only yesterday what a truly brilliant singer Martha is and how everything would be solved if only we could have her in the show as the star. You remember that?'

'Perfectly.'

'Well, what I'm about to suggest is - why not *ask* her? There's nothing lost, is there.'

'Great squawks! But - '

'Oh, I know you said you wouldn't dare and maybe I'm brash and don't know my place but - '

'Are you suggesting,' said Fat Martha, 'that *I* should appear in this terrible show of yours?'

'Forgive her,' said Captain Curly, hastily. 'She's new.'

'I've gone too far,' said Fleur, contritely. 'I got carried away. I just thought,' she continued wistfully, 'that it's only *once* and the Commandant might be hurt if she doesn't appear and also the rest of us could get some sleep knowing the show was in safe hands and - after all, if you're organising a show, you want it to be *good*.'

'Forget it,' said Captain Curly. 'There's a good hen.'

'Yes, I'll forget it. Back to rehearsal. Far end of camp.'

'Now, just you hang on,' said Fat Martha. 'Don't you be so quick. I'm the one who takes the decisions round here and I'm not going to have any show in my camp that isn't perfect. What are you suggesting I do?'

'That would be entirely up to you, of course,' said Captain Curly. 'If you really mean it - '

'When I say a thing I mean it.'

'It would be super to have some of your operatic arias. Six or seven of them - a dozen if you like. We could fit the rest of the stuff around them. Great squawks! I can hardly believe our luck.'

'You don't have much time for rehearsal,' said Fleur. 'Two nights only. Is it possible?'

'Just get out of my way and let me get on with it.'

When Fleur drifted thankfully off to sleep in her little cage it was to the strains of Fat Martha's singing. It was, she thought dreamily, a marvellously strong voice. Fat Martha was in her own quarters but even so her singing could be heard from end to end of the camp. It would easily drown any other sound. It was the perfect voice for the occasion.

The song was *One Fine Day* from *Madame Butterfly*. In Fleur's half-awake state the words became transformed...

One fine day there'll come again
The sound of paws approaching
Beneath the floor
And then we'll all be off out-of-here
And you won't see
Our tail-feathers for du-hu-hust

Meanwhile, every hen not in the scratching party was luxuriating in a good night's sleep. The fox was digging furiously, spurred on by that mental picture of Fat Martha. The earth was flying, the minutes passing. The countdown to freedom had begun.

Tuesday evening:

'Come in, Fleur. Come in, Fleur. Is everything going to plan?'

Squawk.

'Ee are positive there are no problems?'

Squawk.

'Hexcellent. From now on oi shall maintain radio silence unless ee contact me in an emergency. Understood?'

Squawk.

'Good luck, Fleur. The thoughts of free hens everywhere are with ee. Over and out.'

All was running like a well-oiled machine. In the gangway a fresh scratching party, marshalled by Captain Curly, was preparing for a shift.

'Get fell in, the scratching party. Scratchers...scratchers 'SHUN. By the left...'

Fat Martha was singing *They call me Mimi* from *La Bohème*.

* * *

During the afternoon of the next day, Wednesday, the Commandant appeared, accompanied by another human. They walked down the gangway together and at intervals the Commandant pointed to a hen and muttered something. Among the hens thus indicated was Ethel and, straining to overhear what he was saying, Fleur caught the single word 'cull'.

Ethel heard it too. She stared frozenly ahead.

'It's all right, Ethel,' murmured Captain Curly when the humans had gone. She also had heard and understood the word. 'It's always a few days before they carry out sentence. We'll be gone by then. Tonight's the night.'

But Ethel said nothing, merely continued staring.

At least, thought Fleur, there wouldn't be any more talk about staying behind. On the other hand...

It might be just the situation in which Ethel could panic and, attempting to curry favour, betray them all.

Evening:

'Taking a last breather,' leered the fox. His paws were covered with earth. 'I couldn't have another peek at the picture, perhaps? Give me that added boost. No? Never mind. See the real thing soon.'

'Here's power to your forepaws,' said Fleur, trying to keep her voice cheerful, unafraid. The fence would be between them for just a little longer.

Tonight was N-Night. H-Hour and M-Minute were approaching fast.

'See you soon. Without a barrier between us.'

'I'll be waiting.'

Fleur went back inside for a final pre-escape committee meeting. With a few exceptions, morale among the prisoners seemed good. Ethel still hadn't moved or spoken since hearing about the cull. She still had that strange, frozen appearance. Others, that silly young Kylie for instance, looked nervous and edgy. But generally spirits were high.

The committee was in its usual place,

Captain Curly calm, Pankhurst strutting impatiently up and down, Homer philosophical. There was no great ceremony, no stirring speech. Fleur simply nodded.

'Tonight,' she said.

'OK, chaps,' said Captain Curly. 'Show's on. Let's get weaving.'

Chapter 10

THE NIGHT OF THE FOX

'What's going on?' said Fat Martha, soon afterwards.

She'd looked out of her quarters to find the camp bustling. Hens were out of their cages and moving purposefully around. It was enough to put one in a daze. Only a few days before there had been order, efficiency, every hen in its appointed place. How had all this come about?

'Final dress rehearsal,' said Captain Curly. 'Don't worry. We're all off to the far end so we won't disturb you.'

'Oh, I see. Wait a minute, though. If this is a dress rehearsal why aren't I in it?'

'We discussed that, didn't we, chaps, but - '

'We decided,' said Homer, 'that it wouldn't be dignified for you to join in with the *hoi polloi*. Not necessary either.'

'Much better you perfect your own part,' said Captain Curly, 'without being bothered while we put some of the sillier hens through their paces. You know you can't bear stupidity.'

Fat Martha surveyed the scurrying hens.

'All right, but when this show's over we get back to normal. I'm beginning to regret I gave permission but don't think I'm going soft because of it.'

'Just two more nights and you'll be putting the boot in again.'

'I'll say. The glare as well. All right. Clear off. I'm going to gargle.'

Captain Curly waited till there was a raucous rattling sound from Fat Martha's quarters, then gave the nod to Fleur.

Fleur was getting the hens out of their cages and down under the floorboards. Every hen had to be down there, ready and waiting, by the time Fox arrived; and without knowing exactly when that would happen. It was a mammoth operation. *Tap* at every catch with her beak till the beak ached; *hiss* at the hen inside to *push*!

Hens that had never been out of their cages before, that had never expected to know what it was like to be out of their cages till the day of the cull, made their first feeble, tottering steps. They flapped down into the gangway to join the file waiting to drop through the gap in the floorboards and grope their bewildered way, guided by Pankhurst in near total darkness, to the corners furthest from where the scratchers were still tunnelling.

There they huddled, waiting for they knew not what, putting their trust in Fleur and Captain Curly and blindly hoping that when their terror was over they would find themselves at last in the promised land of freedom and life.

Hen after hen after hen. Cage after cage after cage. Tap, tap, tap. *'Push, push, push.'*

'Push,' said Fleur, yet again, without looking, into a cage.

'I *suppose* I'd better come with you,' said the hen inside, fearfully. It was Marilyn. 'Though only because I wouldn't want to stay here on my own. I can't believe in all this grass and sky and stuff and even if they really do exist, I can't see what's so marvellous about them. What's their point?'

'Well, make up your mind and stop gossiping,' said Captain Curly, who happened to be passing. 'The rest of us have work to do.'

Marilyn pushed with a 'what's it matter, anyway?' look.

Tap and tap and tap again...

'Push,' said Fleur to another hen but this time the hen remained immobile. It was Ethel, staring back with that frozen expression.

'Come on, Ethel. We've got to *move*.'

'I can't, Fleur. I'm afraid.'

'All the hens are afraid, Ethel. And if you stay here you'll be on your own and you know what'll happen then. The cull, Ethel. The *cull*.'

Ethel turned her head to one side. There was a nobility about her and Fleur felt suddenly ashamed of ever suspecting that she might betray them.

'I know it here,' said Ethel. 'I feel safe.'

Goodbye, Ethel.
Good luck

There was nothing Fleur could do. 'Goodbye, then, Ethel and good luck,' she said.

Hens by the score, by the hundred, filing down fearfully into the dark, cramped world below the floorboards. Hens that had never known darkness, or even movement.

'Is the tunnel almost through?' they asked each other as they crowded together. 'Is that why we're down here?'

The scratching party heard the activity taking place behind them and didn't understand it at all because they knew they

107

weren't anywhere near through, had no idea when they *would* be through. They were scratching so feebly that it made little impression.

'Just carry on till you're told to stop,' Fleur had told them. 'Trust your committee.'

Every cage but Ethel's was empty now, the great shed deserted save for poor frozen Ethel and for Fat Martha, warbling lustily in her quarters. She was singing the *Habanera* from *Carmen*, stamping and strutting to the rhythm.

'Terrible, isn't it,' said Captain Curly, with a shudder. She and Fleur had just dropped through the gap. 'Let's join the other hens.'

'It's time to tell them,' said Fleur, tautly. 'Scratchers first.'

'Stop scratching?' said the scratchers, puzzled. 'But why? We are not nearly through yet.'

But they did so. They withdrew to join the others, puzzled and afraid.

'Now spread the word,' Fleur said to Captain Curly and Pankhurst and Homer. 'Watch out for panic.'

'I'm not far off it myself,' said Homer.

The news rippled through the mass of hens like a bitterly cold breeze through long grass.

'Fox! The prehistoric monster! He is coming here? Digging his way in now?'

In the first moments it seemed like a betrayal.

'We trusted Fleur,' said some of the frightened hens. 'And you, Captain Curly. We believed in you. Now there will be a massacre.'

'It's the only way,' said Captain Curly. 'Trust us still. We need Fox's digging ability. We would never get out of here without him. And if you are totally silent he will not see you here in the darkness. Fleur is trained to deal with him.'

'Trust Fleur,' said Pankhurst, eyes shining. 'She is a technological hen, greater even than the great Ermintrude. Have faith in her.'

'When Fox comes,' said Fleur, 'leave him to me. All you must do is file through the tunnel he has dug to freedom.'

'And now silence,' said Fleur. 'We must be able to hear a feather drop.'

'But Fleur,' said Captain Curly, quietly, 'will we really be all right?'

'I have my gun. With two pellets.'

'Are you sure it will work?'

'I hope so. But now we must be silent, too.'

The minutes passed. And then an hour while the hens stayed silent and petrified. And a fear grew steadily in Fleur's own breast; that Fox would not come after all or that he would not come before daylight - and Fleur's sense of time told her that dawn could not now be far away; that she would have to send all the hens back to their cages; that Fat Martha would finish her practice and find the empty cages and the gap in the floorboards and raise her beak to the alarm cord...

There was the faintest of sounds. Fleur, recognising it for what it was, moved towards it. Every other hen watched and marvelled. It was possible to see her outline faintly against the light filtering through the gap in the floorboards.

'Ermintrude!' murmured Pankhurst, over-come with admiration.

The earth stirred. Paws and a snout appeared, shaking off soil. Then Fox was coming out of the hole and prehistory like a dinosaur springing to life again. Innumerable eyes were fixed on him, just able to make him out though he couldn't see them.

All of him was out now, crouched in the narrow space between earth and floorboards.

'Hello,' said Fleur. 'You kept your promise.'

His teeth gleamed white. There was no fence between them now.

'And you yours. It's too squashed to be comfortable down here. Take me to my love.'

'This way. Up through the gap in the floorboards. You don't mind if I keep my distance...'

The teeth gleamed again. 'You are quite safe.'

Yes. Probably. Until she had shown him Fat Martha, anyway. All she had to do now was get him through the gap and then trap him there by quickly pulling the floorboard back in place. While he was busy with Fat Martha, giving her her just desserts, the prisoners could start making their escape through the tunnel. Ethel was still up there, too, but she, though no doubt terrified, would be safe in her cage. And when he'd finished with Fat Martha she would be perfectly capable of preventing him from getting below again, even if he were able to shift the floorboard by himself which he probably wasn't...

Yes, just get him through the gap...that was all that was needed...except...

Except that she had experienced a sudden pang of horror. Not for herself or for the other hens but...

For Fat Martha.

She'd been deluding herself. She couldn't do it. However much Fat Martha deserved to die, as a traitor to her fellow hens, Fleur could not bring herself to be the agent of that death.

She was not ruthless enough. She could not throw off her civilised upbringing on Stringroundknees Farm. And she hated

herself for it because she knew that by
hesitating she was putting every prisoner in
her charge at risk.

As she stood immobile, somewhere in the
darkness a hen made a slow, agonised
clucking sound. It was a sound of terror that
the hen had been unable to hold back any
longer.

The fox looked sharply round; suddenly to sense and become aware of those eyes watching from the far recesses. In an instant there was an outburst of clucking and screeching. Panic. Silence became pandemonium and there the great escape might have ended in chaos and massacre if Fat Martha had not at that moment stuck her beak down through the gap in the floorboards and squawked, though the words were heard by no hen.

'What's going on? What are you horrible lot doing down here making all that racket?'

It ended in a long, gurgling squawk of horror as she found herself looking into the eyes of Fox.

Only the narrowness of the gap saved her as Fox, who had been about to slide towards the other hens, suddenly jack-knifed and leapt exultantly after her. By the time he had squeezed and wriggled through, Fat Martha was flapping panic-stricken along the gangway.

As suddenly as it had been broken, silence fell again beneath the floorboards.

'Get the hens out,' Fleur screeched to Captain Curly.

'Pull the floorboard back over the hole,' Captain Curly squawked back. 'Quickly. You've got him.'

But Fleur didn't do that.

Instead, she scrambled up through the gap.

'Come back!' screeched Captain Curly, losing her control for the first and last time ever. But Fleur was already pushing the floorboard back into place with her claw. She was alone with Fox and Fat Martha, save for Ethel petrified in her cage. Fox was charging along in triumphant pursuit.

'Fox!' she squawked. 'Fox! Stop!'

He glanced round. In Fleur's claw was her gun.

'I am Free-Ranging Fleur, Special Agent of the Resistance. I have a gun and I won't hesitate to use it.'

The fox stopped; sat down; and laughed. While only just behind him, within reach of an outstretched paw, Fat Martha squashed herself against the wall and froze into a petrified mass.

'Now that really is funny,' said the Fox. 'I won't be able to get my jaws round Fat Martha, even more desirable in the flesh though she is, for laughing. I shall have to steady myself.'

'There was a fox who laughed once before, a long time ago. Have you ever heard the legend of Ermintrude and the Fox?'

'Can't say I have. It sounds silly. What are you going to do with that thing in your claw?'

'Shoot you. It's like a human's shotgun. It works from a distance. Though this one won't kill you, just knock you out for hours till the humans find you.'

'Oh dear, oh dear, oh dear! Since you're so human I'll be asking you for a hanky to wipe my eyes with next. Even if that thing in your hand works your claw's so stiff and trembling you couldn't hit a barn door '

It was true that her claw was stiff and shaking.

' - so I suppose I'd better try to stop laughing and deal with you before it steadies. I'll have Fat Martha for pudding.'

'Shoot him, Fleur!' squawked Fat Martha, suddenly finding voice again. 'Fleur, if I've ever given offence I apologise - '

'Oh, do shut up, Fat Martha. I don't know why I'm bothering to save you - '

The fox advanced, leering.

Fleur fired.

There was a terrible cry. Not from Fox but from Fat Martha. The pellet had hit her. She keeled over.

'What did I tell you!' laughed the fox. He was close to her now, his great grinning jaws filling the whole world in front of her. She fired again, her only remaining pellet.

He winced while still laughing. It must have hit him but he kept coming on. Perhaps he was too powerful for the pellet to have any effect. She tried to squirm out of reach and saw the petrified face of Ethel, watching. . . .

Chapter 11

WHAT HAPPENED IN THAT CRIMSON-GOLD DAWN

When the Commandant arrived some time later he found a strange scene.

A fox lay unconscious on the floor, mouth open, almost as if it had been laughing. In a nearby cage lay Fat Martha, also unconscious. Another hen was in its cage, frozen and staring and apparently in a state of shock. Otherwise the shed was empty.

Further investigation revealed that a floorboard was out of place and that a newly dug tunnel, clearly the work of the fox, ran from beneath the floorboards to a point outside the boundary fence. A small bag containing strange objects was found in a cage.

The baffled and furious Commandant brought members of his staff to the scene to discuss the situation. There was speculation that the fox had dug his way in, managed to force a floorboard and then eaten every hen in the place but two. This feat would no doubt have led to unconsciousness. However, it seemed hardly possible for various reasons, apart from the fact that the hens had been securely caged.

The entrances to both shed and compound were left open while this debate was going on and the fox, reviving, seized the opportunity to slink out, so anxious to be gone that he didn't spare a glance for Fat Martha.

Fat Martha herself also came to shortly afterwards and she too fled, fearing that her chances of living to a ripe and contented old age as a collaborator were no longer high. What happened to her is not known. Perhaps she still sings and stamps the *Habanera* in some remote hide-out but, again, the chances are not high.

Ethel was taken away soon afterwards. It is better not to dwell on that. But, anyway, we are getting ahead of ourselves.

*   *   *

Fleur had been the last hen through the tunnel.

With his jaws almost around her the fox had faltered, staggered and sunk down, slipping into unconsciousness.

Fleur had taken a moment to recover then she had pushed Fat Martha into a cage, in case the fox inconveniently recovered consciousness again. She had then despairingly and fruitlessly given Ethel a last chance to come with her before slipping back down through the floorboards and pulling the loose one into place again.

She had joined the last of the stragglers, the most nervous of the hens being pushed and bullied through the tunnel by Pankhurst who was determined not to let them 'chicken out.'

And now they were all through, every last hen of them, out in the world they had never really believed in; a world revealed in all its splendour as the sky they hadn't really believed in brightened in the east and the sun they hadn't really believed in came tipping over the horizon in a lovely crimson-gold dawn.

It was now up to Fleur to guide them to the freedom and safety of Stringroundknees Farm: to a human, only a short distance; to a newly-released prisoner a journey of untold dangers, a trek into prehistory with wonders and monsters all about.

'Forward!' cried Fleur.

This is no glib tale of easy victory and happiness ever after. Many hens died in that lovely crimson and gold dawn. Some were taken by the foxes that got into the column and ran amok before being driven off by the sound of shotgun fire from Stringroundknees Farm where stood what appeared to be a heap of old waterproof clothing with a clay pipe sticking out from where a mouth might be.

Some of the hens panicked and ran off, never to be seen again. Some were simply too weak to stagger on and lay down to suffer whatever fate might befall them.

Marilyn's fate was as sad as any. She came out of the tunnel and felt the breeze on her

feathers and stood open-beaked in that
shimmering dawn, dazzled by the rays of the
sun. And now she knew not only that sun
and sky and green grass truly did exist, as
did the sounds of the birds singing and the
ripple of the water in the stream by her side,
but that they were more wonderful than

That lovely, crimson-gold dawn

anything she could ever have dreamed of.

And as she stood enchanted, a fox seized her and carried her off in that lovely, shimmering, crimson and gold dawn. She had had to do all her living within moments.

Fleur, at first dashing around in relief and triumph at having successfully completed the great escape, was suddenly overcome by feelings of guilt and remorse as she realised that, for many, it was leading only to suffering and death.

Stumbling upon a hen lying exhausted on the grass she tried to help her with her claw, the claw that had made her special. But it was of little use now.

'You can't drag me all the way to safety,' said the hen, watching her. 'It's impossible even for a hen like you. It's no use trying.' Fleur noticed that she had been eating grass. There was a little blade of it in her beak. And there was mud on her claw.

'But a fox will get you,' said Fleur, despairingly, 'or another of what you think of as monsters. With you so close to safety. And it will be my fault for bringing you out of the camp into this world which for you is only brutal and cruel. You haven't tasted life yet.'

'Yes, I have,' said the hen. 'It's here in my beak. You've no need to feel guilty, Fleur. There can be no real joy without pain and risk. Death is as much part of life as the mud on one's claw and the sun on one's tail-feathers. I go happily with this blade of grass in my beak. Now go save yourself because there's nothing more you can do for me. But thank you for what you've already done.'

It was Kylie.

'Mission completed,' Fleur said to the dark shape in the woodshed. She saluted with the melancholy nonchalance of one who has known action, who has lived on the edge.

'To my entire satisfaction,' said S.

'I had to leave some equipment behind.'

'It can be replaced.'

Fleur had said farewell to Captain Curly, Pankhurst, Homer and the others. There had been no emotion, just a crisp 'We'll remember these times, won't we, Fleur,' from Captain Curly, a devoted 'It's been an honour to serve under you,' from Pankhurst and a respectful 'You will become a modern legend,' from Homer. Then they had gone, taken away to free farmyards throughout the country.

She would never forget them. They had endured much together. Nor would she forget poor Ethel.

'It might interest ee to know,' said S, 'what's in the press about it.' There was a rustling and the feeble light from the grimy window was almost obscured altogether as a newspaper was held close to it. A pair of spectacles appeared above the pipe.

'There's a liddle bit in the *Times* says: "The mass escape from Cold Ditch has led to specu- specuculation - that a secret undercover operation able to call on vast resources is at work. Government sources today refused to comment" and...'

There was more rustling of paper.

'The *Sun*'s got an exclusive. A giant picture of Fat Martha. It says "The mincing, brutal, conceited Fat Martha kept this picture by her perch, no doubt to gloat and slobber over her own evil appearance. This monstrous hen has now fled, believed to be hiding out in the hope of returning one day..." but ee don't want to hear all this, Fleur.'

The newspapers were lowered.

'Time ee had a rest. But not for long, Fleur. The struggle is only just beginning. Freedom needs ee endlessly.'

Free-ranging Fleur saluted again and turned smartly on her claw. It was time for a chat with Betty, a woodlouse and the Music Club. A song ran through her head:

> *We'll meet again*
> *Don't know where, don't know when*
> *But I say to every hen we'll meet again*
> *Some sunny day.*